Nikki and the Rocking Horse

BY ALAN BROWN

ILLUSTRATED BY PETER UTTON

Collins

An imprint of HarperCollinsPublishers

For Nicola
A.B.

To the Bethnal Green
Museum of Childhood
P.U.

First published in hardback in Great Britain by HarperCollins Publishers Ltd in 1998
First published in Picture Lions in 1999
3 5 7 9 10 8 6 4 2
ISBN: 0 00 664 517-8

Picture Lions is an imprint of the Children's Division, part of HarperCollins Publishers Ltd,
77-85 Fulham Palace Road, Hammersmith, London W6 8JB.

Text copyright © Alan Brown 1998
Illustration copyright © Peter Utton 1998
The author and illustrator assert the moral right to be identified
as the author and illustrator of the work.

Printed and bound in Singapore by Imago.

Once upon a time there was a toy shop, and a rocking horse and a little girl called Nikki who wanted the rocking horse.

The toy shop was full of wonderful wooden toys. There were trucks and dolls and acrobats, painted bright shiny red, custardy yellow and grassy green. There were smooth glossy eggs, bricks and birds in grainy brown wood, polished and gleaming.

Nikki pressed her nose flat against the cold glass window.
She screwed up her eyes and squinted till her head ached.
She could see past the bright lights of the window, past the
wonderful wooden toys in bright shiny colours and into the
dimness of the shop.

There at the back, where it could not possibly leap to freedom, was a proud and prancing rocking horse. Its eyes were wide and its nostrils flared. It had a tasselled mane and a red leather saddle, strong wooden legs and runners, and a sweeping swishing tail.

It was the most wonderful horse in the world.

Nikki pulled Mum into the toy shop and the toy maker showed them his wonderful rocking horse. He lifted Nikki into the horse's saddle. He put Nikki's feet in the stirrups and put the reins in her hands. Then he made a "Giddy-up!" sort of noise.

The rocking horse plunged down on its back legs and waved its hooves in the air. Then it plunged down on its front legs and kicked up its heels. It seemed to shake itself and give a great neighing squeak of its runners. Then it galloped. It galloped so fast that the toy shop seemed to be flying past. The wooden soldiers stood to attention, the dolls waved and all the cars and buses stopped to let Nikki gallop by.

Nikki got down from the rocking horse. Her legs were wobbly.

"It knows how to gallop," she said.

"It's a lovely horse," said Mum, "but it costs a lot of money."

Nikki wanted the rocking horse more than anything. Every time they passed the toy shop she dragged Mum in, and the toy maker sat her on the horse, and they galloped. And while Nikki galloped Mum always sold a toy to somebody. She was very good at selling things.

One day as they left the toy shop Mum said, "I can't afford to buy you expensive toys, but I might be able to make them. The toy maker runs a woodwork class, and I've joined!"

So every Wednesday from then on, Gran came to baby-sit and Mum went to her class. It was fun being with Gran, but Nikki was always thinking about the toys Mum might be making.

At the woodwork class, Mum was making a rocking horse as a surprise for Nikki.

The first week Mum cut the horse on its runners out of sweet smelling wood. She glued and clamped it together and left it to stick.

The second week Mum smoothed the horse's body with a file and sandpaper. Before she came home she just had time to varnish the wood.

The third week Mum painted the horse golden yellow, with splodgy black spots and startled eyes. She fixed a hairy mane and bushy tail to the body, and painted the runners blue.

Mum was so clever!

By the fourth week the paint was dry. Mum attached the reins and the saddle and stirrups.

At last the rocking horse was ready! Mum wanted to try it, but she was too big.

The toy maker looked a bit puzzled, but Mum wrapped the horse up before he could say anything.

That night Nikki watched from her bedroom window for Mum to come home. A little blue van pulled up at the door. Mum and the toy maker carried a huge parcel into the house. They made a lot of noise going "Shhhh!" and giggling, but Nikki was awake anyway. She had been waiting for them.

"I've got a surprise for you!" Mum said next morning. "Come and see!"

Nikki pulled the brown paper off the surprise. She climbed on and leaned forwards and backwards, kicked her heels and said, "Giddy-up!"

Nothing happened. It was a horse that wouldn't gallop.

"It's a bit wonky," Mum admitted. "There's something not quite right."

"It doesn't gallop," said Nikki.

The next day Nikki and Mum went back to the toy shop to find the secret of galloping.

The toy maker lifted Nikki on to his proud wooden rocking horse. Nikki put her feet in the stirrups and took the reins in her hands. Then she made a "Giddy-up!" sort of noise. The rocking horse plunged down on its back legs and waved its hooves in the air. Then it plunged down on its front legs and kicked up its heels. It seemed to shake itself and give a great neighing squeak of its runners. Then it galloped.

It seemed to gallop three times round the toy shop before Nikki could blink. It galloped past the toy maker, past Mum, past the customers in the shop. Nikki hung on to the rocking horse's mane and her own hair streamed out behind her.

"Neigh, neigh!" went the squeak of its runners.

"Hooray!" shouted the customers.

When she was quite out of breath, Nikki pulled on the reins and the horse came to a stop, in exactly the place where they had started.

Nikki got down from the rocking horse. Her legs were wobbly.

"It knows just how to gallop," she said.

"I'm sorry," said Mum miserably. "I've sold it. I've sold the rocking horse to the lady and gentleman."

Nikki just looked.

"I had to," Mum said, "they've got the money. Their daughter fell in love with the horse when she saw it gallop."

Mum held Nikki very tight and they both cried.

Later that day the toy maker came to tea. He looked at the rocking horse that Mum had made.

"It doesn't gallop," said Nikki.

The toy maker smiled and said, "Maybe I can fix it. I'm good at making toys, but I'm not good at selling them."

"Mum's good at selling them," said Nikki.

"That's right," said the toy maker. He looked at Mum and said, "Would you like to work in the shop, selling toys, while I get on with making them? We could be partners."

Mum went bright red, but Nikki could tell she was pleased.

"And you'll fix my rocking horse?" Nikki asked.

"Of course," said the toy maker. "But I'll do that anyway."

And that's what happened. The toy maker got
on doing what he did best – making toys – and
Mum did what she did best – selling the toys in
the shop. Nikki helped, by playing with the toys.

Nikki played with the trucks and dolls and
acrobats, painted bright shiny red, custardy
yellow and grassy green. She played with the
smooth glossy eggs, bricks and birds in grainy
brown wood, polished and gleaming. She played
with any of the toys she liked.

The toy Nikki loved best of all was her rocking horse at home, the rocking horse that Mum made and the toy maker fixed. The rocking horse that nobody would ever, could ever buy.

She climbed on and made a "Giddy-up!" sort of noise. The rocking horse plunged down on its back legs and waved its hooves in the air. Then it plunged down on its front legs and kicked up its heels.

The horse seemed to shake itself and give a great neighing squeak of its runners.

Then it galloped, and galloped, and galloped.

First published in Great Britain by HarperCollins Publishers Ltd in 1998
1 3 5 7 9 10 8 6 4 2
ISBN: 0 00 198126 9
Text copyright © Alan Brown 1998
Illustration copyright © Peter Utton 1998
The author and illustrator assert the moral right to be identified
as the author and illustrator of the work.
A CIP catalogue record for this title is available from the British Library.
Printed and bound in Singapore.